Faber
Stories

Alan Bennett has been a leading dramatist since *Beyond the Fringe* in the 1960s. His works include *Talking Heads*, *Forty Years On*, *The Lady in the Van*, *A Question of Attribution*, *The Madness of George III* (and the Oscar-nominated screenplay), an adaptation of *The Wind in the Willows*, *The History Boys*, *The Habit of Art*, *People*, *Hymn* and *Cocktail Sticks*. He has also written prose collections: *Writing Home*, *Untold Stories* (PEN/Ackerley Prize, 2006) and *Keeping On Keeping On*; and produced a poetry anthology, *Six Poets, Hardy to Larkin*. Fiction includes *The Uncommon Reader* and *Smut: Two Unseemly Stories*.

Alan Bennett

The Shielding of Mrs Forbes

Faber Stories

ff

First published in this single edition in 2019
by Faber & Faber Limited
Bloomsbury House
74–77 Great Russell Street
London WC1B 3DA
First published in *Smut* in 2011

Typeset by Faber & Faber Limited
Printed and bound by CPI Group (UK) Ltd, Croydon, CR0 4YY

The right of Alan Bennett to be identified as author of this work
has been asserted in accordance with Section 77 of the Copyright,
Designs and Patents Act 1988

A CIP record for this book
is available from the British Library

ISBN 978–0–571–35182–4

MIX
Paper from
responsible sources
FSC® C020471
www.fsc.org

10 9 8 7 6 5 4 3 2 1

Like many a handsome man, Graham Forbes had chosen to marry someone not nearly as good looking as himself and even slightly older.

'Chucked himself away if you ask me,' his mother said. Which of course, he didn't. 'Waste, waste, waste. I'm his mother. I'm good looking. Naturally one assumed he'd marry someone along the same lines. We've always been so close.'

'My chum' she called him. 'My young man'.

'We told each other everything. Or I thought we did.'

Graham's father having nothing to say, said nothing.

'I feel such a fool putting the announcement in the paper. I mean, "Betty".

'What sort of a name is that? Margaret, yes. Joan, possibly. Though I must confess Caroline was the least I'd been hoping for. But Betty!'

As names one might think Betty and Graham nicely matched, both dull and unassertive and not committing their bearers to any particular stance on human affairs in the way that Tessa does, or Rory even. But this was partly the trouble. For, though she could never admit it, Graham's mother blamed herself for calling him Graham in the first place. In the years since he was born her sights had risen and Graham was not nearly the classy name she'd once thought. She wished now that she could get rid of it as she had got rid of the dark oak dining suite that belonged to the same period. But though car-boot sales exist to dispose of discarded aspirations there are no stalls dealing in our most unwanted commodities like names, relatives or one's own appearance in the glass.

'I wouldn't care,' said Graham's mother, 'but her first name's only the half of it. Look at her second name: Green. Betty Green. I wouldn't put it past her to be Jewish. I've known Green be a Jewish name.'

'It's actually Greene,' said Graham's father. 'Like the novelist. There's a silent "e".'

Graham's father was understandably sensitive to this spelling, being something of a silent he himself. Indeed his wife was often taken for a widow. She had so much the air of a woman who was coping magnificently that a husband still extant took people by surprise.

'I believe he's a Catholic.'

'Who?' said Graham's mother.

'Greene. The novelist. It comes up in his books from time to time.'

'Oh,' said his wife. 'I wouldn't want my son marrying a Catholic.'

For Graham's mother there was little to choose between Jews and Catholics. The Jews had holidays that turned up out of the blue and the Catholics had children in much the same way.

'I suppose she could be a Catholic,' said Graham's father. 'I could see her as a nun.' The idea seemed to please him but it didn't please his wife.

'Just our luck she missed her vocation. I mean face facts, Edward. He's very good looking; she isn't. Marriage is supposed to be a partnership. Good-looking people marry good-looking people and the others take what's left.'

'There's always love,' said Mr Forbes lamely.

'Love,' snorted Mrs Forbes. 'Of course there's

love. She's in love with him, who wouldn't be? But what does he see in her?'

'She may have money.'

'A hole in her cardigan and the same tights three days running? I've seen no sign of it.'

'Her parents are dead.'

'That doesn't stop her going to the dry cleaners. If only she'd had some parents we'd have a better idea.'

'She does have parents,' Mr Forbes pointed out patiently. 'Everyone has parents. It's just that hers are both dead.'

'So she claims,' said Mrs Forbes. 'They probably took one look and abandoned her on a hillside somewhere, the way they do in stories. Orphans, I don't trust them. Didn't we see something like that at the Playhouse?'

'*Oedipus*,' said Mr Forbes. 'Only that was ancient Greece. This is Alwoodley.'

'Ancient Greece? They were wearing suits,' Mrs Forbes said. 'He was in a sports car.'

'That was the production,' said Mr Forbes.

'And he had a mobile phone.'

Mr Forbes gave up the struggle and switched to silent mode.

Mrs Forbes's suspicions notwithstanding there was no mystery about Betty's origins. Betty was a genuine orphan, her parents both having died when she was in her teens. So far as the marriage was concerned she was trying not to think about them too much: they might have liked Graham; they would certainly have liked his father; it was with his mother they would have drawn the line.

'I'm going to feel such a fool on the wedding day,' said his mother. 'And to think I've looked forward to it ever since the day he was born. He's always been so fastidious. I've known him spend half an hour choosing a tie. And he has no end of shoes. It's such a waste. And God knows what the children will be like.'

'I suppose . . .' mused Mr Forbes.

'You suppose what?'

'I suppose they've . . . had it off.'

'I beg your pardon?'

'Done it. Got his leg over.'

There was a pained silence. It was an ancient battleground . . . what she called it, what he called it and whether he was allowed to call it anything at all.

'I suppose you mean "made love". Because I prefer not to think of it.'

'She's probably', said Mr Forbes, warming to the fray, 'a bit of a goer.'

'A goer? Edward. When are you going to learn that there are certain phrases you cannot use?'

'I've heard Graham use it.'

'Graham is different. Graham is young, attractive and drives a sports car. He has a life with the top down and language to match. He can say "guy" and "bird" and "cool", all the things young people say. You can't. I heard you say "tits" the other night at the Maynards'. You're too old to say "tits".'

'What age is that? When is the cut-off point? How old does one have to be still to say tits?'

'It's not just a question of age. Some people can say it all their lives. Whereas you, you've never had enough dash.'

'Oh. Dash is it now?'

'Dash. Flair. Brio. All the qualities that come to Graham naturally.'

The irony was that though Graham's father was much less particular about whom his dashing son chose to marry, like his wife he would have been much happier if Graham had not married at all, though for different reasons. Graham married would leave his father in the entirely undiluted company of his mother, a prospect he dreaded and that she was now envisaging too.

'With Graham gone at least we will have the chance to get to know one another again. You could introduce me to this internet you're always buried in. After all, life is for living.'

Mr Forbes who had just made a new and unseemly friend in Samoa saw all his cautious little world about to be kicked over.

He shut the door carefully and settled in front of the screen. Better make the most of it. And here at least he could say tits.

When Mr Forbes wondered if Betty had money he was right. She did. And Graham knew because he worked in a bank.

'He does not work in a bank,' said Graham's mother. 'He is in banking.'

He had met Betty when she had come in for advice after her father died.

'These what you call shares,' said Betty, 'Dad seems to have quite a collection. There's even some from Japan.'

'This is the stock market, Miss Greene,' said Graham. 'It is not philately. Let me be the first to congratulate you. You are a rich woman. Bereavement apart, you are laughing.'

'I don't understand,' said Betty, who understood perfectly well but thought how nice his hands were.

'Would you like me to explain?' said Graham.

'If it's no trouble,' said Betty.

To be taken in by this degree of ingenuousness one has to be pretty ingenuous oneself.

'He's such a straightforward boy,' said his mother. 'I blame myself.'

One does not have to be in the forefront of the struggle for women's rights to find Betty's decision to marry Graham deplorable. She wasn't wholly infatuated, though she liked the way he looked; but, so too did he and that unfatuated her a bit. Still, she could be forgiven for thinking that her money entitled her to someone out of her own league. Besides she liked her maiden name no more than her future mother-in-law did. It was time for a change.

Handsome as he was, for Graham their association was not without its humiliations. He drove, as has been said, a sports car and if it was being serviced his garage lent him an old Ford Escort. Drawn up in his vehicle at the traffic lights Graham was painfully aware of the pitying looks of other drivers.

They were the same looks he got, he imagined, when he went out with the plainish Betty and it was to avoid such embarrassment (and because he was very fond of his car) that made much of what Graham's mother called 'their courting' both nocturnal and motorised.

They were parked in a beauty spot.

'Your mother blames me,' said Betty, undoing his belt.

'She'll get over it,' said Graham lifting himself up in the car seat so that she could ease down his pants. 'After we're married I think we should have a joint account.'

'What's that?' asked his wife-to-be and though this was supposed to be the first one she'd seen she meant the account.

'It's just an arrangement so's you won't have to come running to me for money every five minutes.'

'And the reverse,' thinks Betty. 'Kiss?'

'To begin with,' said Graham, 'then just sort of use your imagination.'

Betty having no parents to make the arrangements for her it fell to Mrs Forbes to oversee the preparations of the wedding, a burden which she shouldered reluctantly, only too conscious of its tragic irony. Still she felt a church ceremony was essential if only to demonstrate that the bride was neither pregnant nor Jewish. But that an occasion to which she claimed to have looked forward half her life should turn out to be a public humiliation seemed almost a punishment.

'I can just see the looks on their faces,' she complained to the dressing-table mirror. Weddings were critical occasions and had to be carried off. Though hardly popular she had a wide circle of like-minded friends, many of whom would be only too pleased to see her discomfited, and a tear ran down her cold-creamed face. Mr Forbes, sitting up in his pyjamas with his laptop felt a pang of sympathy, though it was soon dispelled.

'Have you talked to Graham?'

'Not yet.'

'Not yet? What sort of a father are you?'

'It has to be in church, I suppose?'

It was a question no one had thought to put to the bride though Betty and to some extent Graham would have been quite happy with the registry office. But mindful of his mother and also of the presents Graham thought they should make the effort.

'At least it's not a white wedding,' said Mrs Forbes, heaving herself into bed. 'She's so dark people might think she was Asian.'

'If it has to be in church,' said Mr Forbes, 'I hope it will be in accordance with the Book of Common Prayer.'

'What else should it be in accordance with?' said Mrs Forbes. *'The Highway Code?'*

'It may have escaped your notice,' said her husband, 'but the services these days are different. For a start one has to shake hands with one's neighbour.'

'In my recollection,' said Mrs Forbes, 'one seldom had a neighbour. There were only ever about four people there.'

'Then they'll have to go at least twice because of the banns. I hope . . .' said Graham's father (and this time choosing his words carefully), 'I hope they know the facts of life.'

'Graham is twenty-three.'

'That won't deter Canon Mollison.'

The vicar was old. The chief love of his life was the steam engine, and his version of the facts of life which he had been dispensing over many years relied heavily on the piston, the furnace and the eccentric rod, helpful did one want to travel from

London to Darlington but no preparation for the rigours of modern marriage.

Mr Forbes seldom saw his son on his own. They had never been out for a drink together, for instance, or to a football match as fathers and sons are supposedly wont to do. Graham was so much his mother's child that the father tended to think of him if not quite as his mother's agent then certainly her roving reporter and so was always somewhat wary in his presence. Morning suits being in order Mrs Forbes sent the pair of them off to Moss Bros to get kitted out. It was an awkward occasion made more so by it being assumed that as father and son they would be happy to share a dressing room.

A shy man, Mr Forbes had seldom seen his son undressed since he was a boy and even more seldom had Mr Forbes allowed himself to be so seen. The suits in question were hung up waiting and Graham, emboldened by the presence of several full-length mirrors briskly stripped down to his underpants. Mr Forbes was more tentative and it was only when he was reluctantly in his shirt tails that he found his dress trousers had gone missing. So while they were located he sat miserably on a bench feeling both wizened and portly and tucking his veinous legs as far as he could well out of view. It was an unnecessary precaution as Graham scarcely noticed his father, altogether absorbed in his several reflections and the trousers which he felt were too loose to be properly becoming. It was at this point with Graham standing in front of the mirror arranging and re-arranging his genitals that Mr Forbes remembered his wife's instructions.

'Your mother thinks that you and Betty should go and see the vicar.'

'What for?' Graham put his hand down his trousers to try dressing on the left.

Mr Forbes looked down at his inadequate legs. He needed to ask if his son and his fiancée had made love but since his son was his wife's representative he phrased it accordingly.

'Has the engagement been consummated?'

'Frequently.'

'Your mother says you mustn't tell the vicar that.'

'I imagine he'll have the good manners not to ask.' Mr Forbes looked away as Graham took off his trousers, unashamedly loosening his crotch in the process. Actually the truth was they hadn't done it yet, though they'd done just about everything else but he was unlikely to say that to the vicar or to his mother either.

Mr Forbes's trousers now arrived and with them a greater degree of parental boldness.

'If you are getting married in church, Graham, the vicar likes you to pretend you believe in God. Everyone knows this is a formality. It's like the air hostess going through the safety drill. God's in His heaven and your life jacket's under the seat.'

'I don't see what that's got to do with whether we've done it or not.'

'When you are as old as Canon Mollison,' Mr Forbes said patiently, 'one of the few perks of the job is talking to young people about the sexual act. What in any other context would probably get him arrested, in the vestry passes for spiritual advice.'

'It must be a very depressing job,' said Graham.

15

Still, he looked wonderful and reluctantly taking leave of the mirror he briefly inspected his father. He would do.

So in due course Graham and Betty went to church and the banns were read and they had the session with the vicar. When they came out Betty burst out laughing, which she had been wanting to do inside (Graham had just been bored). Now she made Graham see the funny side of it so that Graham, who had never come across a woman who made jokes, realised, almost for the first time, that he might actually like her.

On the night before his wedding Graham was in bed with a youth called, he thought, Gary. Gary was well built. His smooth flesh was cool, hard and perfectly proportioned, and contemplating the silent back Graham decided it was like the flesh of heroes as described in classical mythology.

'And they didn't have much in the way of small talk either,' mused Graham. 'No,' he said.

'Mmm?' murmured the youth, half-asleep.

'Just thinking aloud,' said Graham. Was his

name not Gary but Trevor? Graham tried half-saying the name to himself. No response. The smooth back rose and fell. Of course many people (many boys he meant) didn't thank you for saying their name. In these circumstances, names tended to be left off along with everything else.

Gary stroke Trevor had a silver chain round his neck from which hung a thin, oblong medallion. It lay now somewhere between his chest and the pillow. It was likely, Graham reasoned, or at least possible that this slip of metal would carry its owner's name, so, stealthily stroking his way to a different district of the vast back he began to edge the medallion round into view. He was relying on the young man being asleep as such a manoeuvre was not easy to disguise, fiddling with someone's identity disc hardly to be incorporated into, or interpreted as, any form of love play known to Graham, though curiosity about everything attached to his companion's person must surely count as a compliment.

Graham lightly lifted the chain free of the young man's neck, and gently pulling it round he eased

it free of a low-lying curl. Even his ears were perfect, at any rate the one he could see, neat, simple,
the lobe furred with a faint, fair down. Slowly the
nameplate edged into view, faintly misted from the
heat of its wearer's body. One side was plain: Graham turned it over.

'Shirley,' the young man said. 'I fuck her on Fridays.'

'Is that nice?' asked Graham.

'She thinks so.'

'Why Fridays?' asked Graham.

'Her hubby plays squash.'

There was a pause while Graham thought about
Shirley and the young man.

'You like that,' said the boy.

'What?'

'Me and Shirley.'

'Why?' said Graham.

'It feels to me you do.'

'Actually,' said Graham, 'I was just looking at your
back.'

'Yeah. I swim. Stroke my bum.'

Graham did so though somewhat abstractedly wishing he could remember the name of its owner. Still, it wouldn't do any harm, Graham decided, to make it plain that he too had irons in other fires.

'I'm getting married in the morning.'

'Ding dong the bells are going to chime,' said the putative Trevor.

'How do you know?' said Graham, who was not into musicals. 'It might have been in a registry office.'

'Allow me to wish you every happiness. Actually, though, not there. Just where my bum joins my legs. It's one of the lesser-known erogenous zones.'

At the word erogenous Graham decided he couldn't be called Trevor and began to lose interest a little.

'In fact,' the young man went on, 'I think I maybe discovered it. If my bum were an orchid it would probably bear my name.'

This was hardly the down-to-earth lorry driver ferrying a load of hard core from Rochdale to Penzance he had earlier claimed to be.

'You seem very articulate for a lorry driver.'

'I read, don't I. In lay-bys. When you see lorries

parked in lay-bys that's what they're doing nine times out of ten. Reading. What's she like? Pretty?'

'No,' said Graham honestly.

'Big tits?'

'Not particularly.'

'Expecting?'

'No.'

'So what're you marrying her for?'

'There are other things,' said Graham primly.

'Oh sure. Don't stop. I like it. It's my favourite thing.'

Graham wearily complied but changed the subject.

'Great flat.'

'Yeah.'

'Quite classy.'

'I like it.'

'And the shower is great.' They had sampled the bathroom earlier. 'Pricey?'

'I manage. So,' and he put his head on his arms, 'no more of this then?'

'Oh, I don't know,' said Graham. 'I shall just have to play it by ear.' See what I can get away with was what he meant. A good deal, he fancied, as the disparity between Betty's looks and his own gave him plenty of room to manoeuvre; it would be some time before she ran out of gratitude; that was only fair.

'I suppose in the circumstances this is your stag night?'

'You could call it that. What kind of lorry is it you drive?'

'A big one.'

'Not a juggernaut, I hope. I disapprove of those on environmental grounds.'

'Well,' said the bum without a name, 'we have to get the goods from Point A to Point B. This time tomorrow night I shall be in Penzance.'

'I shan't.'

'You don't have to stop at my bum. One thing is supposed to lead to another. That's what it's all about. I don't think your mind's on this, Toby. You're thinking of Miss Right.'

Graham wasn't. His thoughts were in the usual place and he was wondering why he should be the one to have to do the stroking.

'On balance,' said the supposed Trevor, 'I prefer it straight. You get through more energy. It's the post-coital rabbit I can't stand. Turn over and I'll do the same for you.'

As Trevor, whose name was actually Kevin but who had said it was Gary, stroked the back of Graham's legs he wondered whether Toby thought this was for free. The question had not been discussed in the bushes where they had met but Kevin which was to say Gary got the feeling that Toby which was to say Graham thought he was doing him the favour and wondered how he might make this misconception plain. Still, as he lightly stroked the underside of his partner's buttocks in the feathery way that he himself preferred he felt a glow of self-satisfaction that he was doing to someone else what he most liked having done to him.

'I don't like that,' said Graham. 'It tickles.'

Abandoning Toby's ticklish bum the young man turned on his back, clasping his hands behind his head. His armpits were top scorers, too, thought Graham, though in what context he could not imagine. Butlin's possibly, or Channel Five.

'Do you like your name?' Graham said.

'Gary?' said Kevin. 'Yes. Yes I do like my name. In fact,' and he raised himself on one elbow and looked down his body, 'I like everything about me. My feet, my belly, my face . . . and, of course, that. I've never had any complaints anyway. And while we're on the subject I think it's about time you did something about that, Toby.'

'All right, Gary,' said Graham, now that the body beside him had a name, feeling his ardour re-kindled, 'what would you like me to do, Gary?'

'Be my guest, Toby,' said Kevin. 'Oh, and in the circumstances, the wedding and so forth, this one's on the house.'

The wedding the following day went off without a hitch, the vicar, having previously noted the disparity in looks between the bride and groom, pronouncing it a most Christian marriage.

The bride's side of the church was only thinly populated even with some of those syphoned off from the overcrowded pews on the groom's side. Betty's parents had been elderly and most of her surviving relatives were elderly too and reluctant to make the journey north. It was unsatisfactory but as Graham's mother reasoned had Betty's family turned out in force it might have confirmed her suspicions about her daughter-in-law's racial ancestry.

There were no bridesmaids, what few women friends Betty had not really bridesmaid material. This was another blessing as the risk with bridesmaids is that they are prone to point up the inadequacies of the bride.

'Not difficult in this case,' thought Mrs Forbes. Or Mrs Forbes senior as she now was.

Where the best man and the ushers were concerned Graham was spoiled for choice and a bevy of high-spirited young men gave the occasion an element of whoopee it might otherwise have lacked.

Still, some of their reactions were unexpectedly heartfelt and at the climax of the service the best man was seen to brush away a tear, a gesture not seen by Mrs Forbes, who was too busy weeping her-

24

self, the happiest couple of all and wholly untearful not Graham and his bride so much as the bride and Mr Forbes, whom she had chosen to give her away. They were radiant.

At the reception both Betty and her new mother-in-law were surprised by what good dancers many of Graham's friends turned out to be even if Graham himself took the floor reluctantly, doing a dutiful round with his mother and then with Betty but thereafter leaving it to his friends, many of whom seemed quite happy to dance on their own.

The unlikely king of the floor, though, was Mr Forbes. He had always been a good dancer; indeed it was one of the reasons why Mrs Forbes had picked him out. These days he seldom got the opportunity to show off his talents but as he waltzed his wife elaborately around the floor it was plain that, despite having overfortified himself with champagne, he had lost none of his skill and together they made an impressive couple.

This was deceptive. The drink had emboldened Mr Forbes and made him uncustomarily combative and he used the freedom of the dance further to explore the permitted limits of his sexual vocabulary.

'Balls?' he quickstepped. 'Scrotum?'

Mrs Forbes stony-eyed gave no indication of having heard but maintained throughout a fixed and ghastly smile as her now foxtrotting partner remorselessly plied her with smut. 'Pussy? Fanny? Arse?'

He might have been murmuring endearments in her ear and it could have been a touching spectacle. Certainly as the number ended the guests broke into spontaneous applause which Mr Forbes acknowledged as holding his wife's hand she gracefully curtseyed. She had never been so unhappy in her whole life.

Having just bought a flat into which they were anxious to move straightaway the happy couple had forgone a lengthy honeymoon in favour of a weekend at a country-house hotel.

What Graham chose to call their 'fooling around' had been virtually unrestrained and surprisingly enjoyable and all with some sort of vehicular setting . . . the front or back seat of the car, his or the more commodious model belonging to his father.

That they had never, in Graham's words again, 'gone all the way' was partly because he was, if only in regard to the opposite sex, quite old-fashioned but also because he had never even in the alternative sphere been into penetrative sex and wanted to put it off as long as possible.

That apart it might be thought strange, his sexual inclinations being what they were, that Graham had never had any worries about the physical side of things. This, though, is to forget how much in love Graham was with himself. True, a mirror was always a help . . . a real mirror, that is; Graham did have his own full-length mirror that travelled with him wherever he went. No one else could see it, of course, but without it he was nothing whereas with it all things were possible: he could have faced a firing squad if he could have watched himself doing it. And though this wasn't quite the spirit in which he approached his wedding night he was looking forward to seeing himself perform. However, when he surveyed their sumptuous quarters in the hotel he realised this was not going to be easy.

In many of the hotel rooms Graham had stayed, not always alone, an artfully located mirror afforded a reflection of the bed, the vision of himself naked on the sheets sufficient in itself to excite him with or without a companion. Here it was plush; grand and lavishly furnished with genuine antiques, the side table piled high with copies of *Country Life*, *Tatler* and *The Field*; one lacquer box contained after-dinner mints, another a selection of the Prince of Wales's biscuits, plus, courtesy of the management, a basket of fruit and a huge bunch of peonies. What there was not was a mirror. There was a massive wardrobe, it's true (bird's-eye maple, French, nineteenth century), but there was no mirror.

Nor were there, as Graham swiftly ascertained while Betty was in the bathroom, any porn channels on the TV. On his travels for the bank Graham was used to staying in hotels a notch or two down from this palatial establishment where, though the accommodation might be less well accoutred, porn was always on offer. There, too, the rooms were smaller and the walls were thinner so that one could sometimes catch the occasional hint of what might be going on next door. Here the swagged drapes, the damasked wall covering, the refectory table, the royal biscuits all proclaimed the establishment's indifference to such unworthy considerations. Honeymoon suite though it might be and the lap of luxury that it certainly was, good taste prevailed and sex was not catered for.

The reflection problem (of which Betty was unaware) was unwittingly solved when hanging up some of her clothes she opened the wardrobe to reveal that the interior of the door was backed by a full-length mirror, so once she was in the bathroom Graham with a little experimentation worked out that fully opened the wardrobe door would give a decent account of what, all being well, would be taking place on the bed.

So when Betty emerged from the bathroom it was to a ready and waiting Graham with the role he chose to play that of the stern and unsmiling husband now at last taking possession of his territory. 'This,' he said as he cast aside his towel, 'this is when the marriage begins in earnest.'

Which it did with Betty abject and submissive and to begin with at any rate their conjunction wholly satisfactory.

Except that as he gazed sideways in admiration at the rise and fall of his buttocks the vigour of the assault caused the wardrobe door to close slightly leaving him with an unappealing reflection of knees and ankles. He twice had to get up and correct this (with no explanation offered to Betty) but when it happened a third time he decided to forget the mirror and just get on with it. From his new wife's point of view this was preferable not simply because she now had her husband's undivided attention but because deprived of the stimulating spectacle of his own heaving buttocks Graham took appreciably longer in reaching a conclusion.

Lying post-coitally naked on the bed Graham considered his wife and himself. He had seen a good many bodies in his young life though few that came up to his own. Since the stakes between him and his partners had seldom been equal, sex generally involved a degree of condescension on Graham's part which in a nicer or less vain man might have been counted as compassion. But not with Graham.

This is where love generally comes in: whether the inequality between the partners is physical or social or indeed financial, evening up the score is what love is about. Still, even in the most perfect of unions there's often detectable an element of bestowal. And that Betty was of the wrong gender made making love to her seem to Graham the greatest bestowal of all. He turned towards her again; it was actually quite enjoyable.

For a marriage that might be thought to have little going for it things actually went very well. It helped that as a cook Betty was good and also inventive; her mother-in-law had been neither so when Graham arrived home from the bank and there was always a delicious meal to be had it was a novelty. Nor did Betty object to him spending the whole of the evening in front of the television; in fact there was very little Betty did object to so that her young husband found himself even more pampered than he had been before.

At work, too, he was prospering, marriage having reassured his superiors at the bank of his seriousness and his dedication and (though this had never been mentioned) his sexual inclinations.

Betty had come along to one or two of the bank-oriented social occasions, grim affairs which she seemed to enjoy and where, out of earshot of Graham, she had impressed his colleagues with the pertinence of her questions: if she was sceptical of the answers she took care not to show it. 'Your good lady seems to have her head screwed on,' said Graham's project manager. 'She's not just a pretty face.' Since she certainly wasn't that Graham took no notice anyway. He did, though, make it plain that he now did not actually need the job which naturally made his superiors all the more eager to offer him a better one.

In other respects too, there was no cause for complaint. Once the novelty had worn off it might have been expected that marital sex could quite soon have lost its charm. Not a bit of it. The truth was Graham found a great deal more to do when making love to Betty than he ever had with the most enterprising of his male partners. Moreover there was a burglarious aspect to doing it with Betty which he had never come across before.

There were the clothes for instance. Had a young man in the past insisted on keeping on his trousers thus leaving Graham to negotiate zip, buttons, pants and whatever else, he would have found the corresponding preliminaries with Betty more familiar. But such slow divestment was an apprenticeship he had never had to serve, his partners gladly casting off whatever they had on the quicker to enjoy Graham's charms. So now, coming home from the bank (and sometimes without even taking off his coat) he gets one in with Betty before supper; he finds the fumbling attendant on her urgent and only partial deshabille particularly exciting as it comes always with the sense that he is breaking in. It's a sense she contrives to give him but Graham is not sophisticated enough to know that. The obstacles were also natural ones bred out of unfamiliarity with the geography of the region and the function of its components. Women, he found himself thinking, had to be investigated. But mouth clamped to mouth while he fumbled around below he had the entirely pleasurable notion that he was cracking a safe. Though he never failed to effect an entry the combination still remained a mystery, with married love for Graham still pleasingly felonious.

If any precautions in the way of condoms and suchlike have gone unmentioned that is a casualty of the storytelling. Though the slithering on of contraceptives has been elided in this narrative, in his premarital sexual sorties Graham had been scrupulous never to omit this preliminary even when giddier bedfellows mocked his circumspection. This, though, should have come as no surprise as however frantic the foreplay the neat fashion in which Graham put his shoes by the bed with his socks tucked inside should have signalled that this was not exactly a free spirit.

However, here again married love had its untransgressive attractions. Since Betty was on the pill or took precautions of her own which Graham did not choose to enquire into, the marital bed was untrammelled by tedious prophylaxis so that what Graham had been expecting to find an onerous and even distasteful duty unexpectedly partook of a freedom and absence of restraint that he found exhilarating. He took to his home sheets with unsheathed abandon; here at least he wasn't going to catch anything and the assurance lent his efforts both confidence and flair. Betty, whose sexual expectations had not been high, found herself the object of prolonged and vigorous and on the whole pleasurable assault. She was astonished at her husband's verve and gusto but if she was astonished there was no one more so than Graham.

Elsewhere Mr Forbes had not been allowed to forget his despicable behaviour at the wedding and he spent several months in more or less permanent exile to the garden shed. In his wife's brief absences from the home he managed to get to his computer and send hurried (and always lying) bulletins to his grass-skirted friend in Samoa. But now he had a new friend.

In the months immediately following their marriage Betty busied herself with furnishing and kitting out the newly bought flat. Firmly rejecting her mother-in-law's offers of help, with Mr Forbes she was more approachable. Though she was herself a dab hand at the computer Mr Forbes was useful in other respects, particularly in locating and shopping for her various requirements. Besides being good company he was also something of a handyman so more and more he could be found making the trip over to his daughter-in-law's where they both shook their heads over their respective partners.

Mr Forbes had retired early, his pension tied to the price of shares in his former company. The resultant fluctuations in his income were a constant source of anxiety to Mr Forbes and finding him often groaning over the stock market Betty eventually persuaded him to tell her why and to take her through his portfolio. Though he felt he was only indulging her curiosity Mr Forbes found Betty surprisingly knowledgeable ('I used to have to do this for my father') and within a few months (and with a lot of laughter) she had so restructured his retirement settlement as to virtually double his income, the only proviso being that he should mention it neither to Graham nor (which was much the same) his mother. Graham's notion of a wife was as an ingenuous dependency and knowing much more than he did she had the sense to keep it quiet. Not for the first time Mr Forbes wondered why a woman so decidedly accomplished had chosen to marry his son.

One of the functions of women, Mr Forbes had long since decided, was to impart an element of trouble into the otherwise tranquil lives of men. His wife, for instance, though almost alarmingly robust, claimed to be seldom altogether well, though it wasn't anything one could put one's finger on. True the trouble was often to do with that department Mr Forbes might have been expected to put his finger on but rarely did while at the same time being something intangible which, unless the man kept it in the forefront of his mind, allowed him to be accused of a lack of consideration and of being heartless. What was wrong, Mr Forbes felt, even with someone as stalwart as his wife was that the man was not perpetually aware that there was something wrong. That was what was wrong. Perhaps Mr Forbes's experience was unfortunate and if this was indeed a flaw of the gender it was one Betty wholly lacked, as she was cheerful, funny and, as Mr Forbes remarked to his wife, 'full of the joys of spring'.

'Who wouldn't be, married to Graham?'

Nor did Betty impose any of the linguistic dos and don'ts which so trammelled frank and open discussion with his wife. 'Balls' figured, 'arse' and the occasional 'Shit!' and greatly daring he even ventured on 'fanny' (at least in its derivative of fannying about). Betty was not in the least put out. Mr Forbes preferred being called Ted but Mrs Forbes thought Ted Forbes sounded like a character in *The Archers* and always called him Edward. Betty, without being told, knew enough about her mother-in-law to call him Edward when she was around and

Ted when she wasn't. It was all part of licensing him to be the bit of a devil he felt his wife had never allowed him to be.

Graham, of course, had been a bit of a devil in his time though if Betty has any inkling of his premarital inclinations she keeps her observations (it would be wrong to call them suspicions) strictly to herself though their life together was not without clues.

Thinking Betty was in the bath Graham was watching a late-night programme on Channel 4 called *Footballers with Their Shirts Off* when she unexpectedly came in on the trail of the hair dryer.

'I didn't know you were interested in football,' said Betty.

'I keep an eye on Newcastle,' said Graham just as (in an old clip) Gary Lineker swapped his shirt with some dish from the former Yugoslavia.

'I prefer him now,' said Betty.

'Who?'

'Gary Lineker,' said Betty. 'Grey hair suits him. Still, nice legs.'

'I wouldn't know,' said Graham primly.

'Funny programme,' said Betty. 'Is it recorded highlights?' and went back to drying her hair.

'Should we have a child?' The question is Betty's and they are in bed.

'Isn't that a bit of a shot in the dark?'

'I wonder about starting a business?'

'What sort of a business?'

'On the internet.' She'd already done this but hadn't said so to Graham.

Graham was silent.

'I have to do something with my life, Graham.'

'You have done something with your life. You've married me. I'm the one who has to do something with his life. Why don't you take up photography?'

Betty sighed.

'Could we go to bed again?'

'Betty. We are in bed.'

'You don't like me to say the word.'

'Make love. Say "make love".'

To say that Betty had entertained no suspicions of Graham's premarital sexual experiences suggests that this is what they were, premarital. This was not entirely true. He still had the odd fling, now more of a treat than it once was partly because it was rarer but also because it was more risky and so seemed to him bolder.

On one of these occasional forays Graham found himself in bed with a well-proportioned young man who, while devoting himself wholeheartedly to the business in hand, still managed to give the impression of being a not unamused spectator.

'So Toby . . .' and the naked young man put his hands behind his head. 'How're you surviving the rigours of married life?'

The question was post-coital and mildly disturbed Graham, who had been smart enough to leave off his wedding ring.

'All right,' he said diffidently.

'All right? All right? I don't like the sound of that. Mind you,' and he looked down at the equally naked Graham, 'I think it's got bigger. Filled out a bit, know what I mean?'

It began to dawn on Graham that they had met

before and the name suddenly came to him. 'Gary.'

'Aww you remembered.' Kevin gave his thigh a squeeze. 'Your stag night, right?'

'You're the long-distance lorry driver.'

'No, no. Your memory is at fault there, Toby. I'm the panel beater.'

'Your hands are very soft for a panel beater.'

'I apply a protective cream.'

It was all coming back to Graham.

'You've gone up in the world.'

'You think so?'

'This place, it's a gated development. Last time you were just in a flat.'

'Nothing but the best,' said Kevin, stroking his belly, 'only Toby – you set too much store by material possessions.'

Not a panel beater, thought Graham. An interior decorator, maybe.

'How's Shirley?'

'Who?'

'Shirley,' said Graham. 'Your girlfriend. You fuck her on Fridays.'

'No such person. I couldn't have anything to do with a girl called Shirley, Friday or any other day of the week. I'm not sure I'd even get it up.'

Graham noted that Gary had exchanged his chain and label for a pair of dog tags.

'These are new,' said Graham.

'Only to you. I like them. They add that whiff of combat. We could be in the Falklands. Or a tent in the Western Desert.'

He was leaning on his left elbow idly tracing a circle round Graham's navel.

This wasn't a scenario Graham had much interest in pursuing. He and Betty had once done it in a tent overlooking Nidderdale, and area of outstanding beauty though it was it had not been a success and a vile tea in Pateley Bridge had not redeemed it.

'I hope you're being diligent and conscientious in the performance of your marital duties. Is she still getting it twice a night?'

Graham who was not dissatisfied with his record in this department smiled complacently.

'She know you play for the opposition?'

'Yes' would have been the prudent answer.

'No,' said Graham. 'No idea.'

'Would she mind, do you think?'

'Of course not,' said Graham, learning from experience. 'Not these days.'

'That's right, Toby. What's gender? Spread it around.'

'Time I was off,' said Graham.

He reached for his clothes neatly folded on the bedside chair.

'Don't fancy a supplementary?'

Graham looked at his watch.

'Can't I'm afraid.'

'She won't mind. Tell her you were kept late at the bank.'

'I didn't say I worked at a bank.'

It's true he hadn't, but casting his mind back he couldn't remember where he'd said he worked. 'You're in a bank. I'm a panel beater. That's how society works. Speaking of which I'm afraid I'm going to have to charge you for this one. Shall we say, £100.'

'A hundred? Fuck me.'

'I wish I could say I just had but that's where you draw the line, Toby, remember?'

'You're lucky I've got it,' said Graham, handing over the notes. 'I don't carry much cash.'

'Why should you?' said Kevin. 'You work in a bank. Nice car.'

Coming away Graham felt uneasy. Had he said he worked at a bank? Had he said which bank? It was this element of risk that was supposed to give these encounters their edge but this time Graham didn't like it one bit.

Besides it was expensive. The gates slid open.

Back in the room Kevin was feeding the number of Toby's new car into his mobile.

For the moment things are looking good for the Forbes family. Graham's marriage is more satisfactory . . . and more satisfying . . . than he could have hoped and he is also making progress at the bank, playing squash with executive clients, sitting in on property deals which, it's true, he doesn't always quite understand but which his wife with a few seemingly naive and common-sense questions helps him to sort out without jeopardising her status as 'the little woman'.

Meanwhile Betty's internet business thrives. For the moment the question of a baby has been shelved though the actual shelves are still being taken care of by Ted, which is to say Mr Forbes senior.

If there is an absentee from this general felicity it is Graham's mother. Naturally she sees much less of Graham married than she did him single. Occasionally he has supper at home if Betty is going out to a concert, say . . . she is a keen music lover . . . a passion she doesn't share with her husband ('I prefer light classical') but which she has communicated to Graham's father who sometimes escorts her, thus leaving mother and son to indulge in their old relationship. But however much she enjoys such occasions they also bring home to Mrs Forbes how empty her life has become.

Once upon a time Mrs Forbes had had hopes of the internet, thinking it would serve as a substitute or, as she put it, 'a hobby'. These hopes, though, have gradually petered out as she has proved persistently incapable of mastering the technology.

'It's really quite simple,' said her teacher, patiently, but since her teacher is her husband he makes sure that essential keys remain unpressed and connections unmade.

'It's a man's game,' he says kindly, which, bearing in mind the use to which he puts it himself, is quite true, the snake-hipped dusky beauty in Samoa (but who actually lives in Clitheroe) safely sequestered from Mrs Forbes's questing but untutored fingers.

Kindlier women than Mrs Forbes might have taken some consolation in an expectation of grandchildren but there seemed to be no sign of them and looking in the mirror and smoothing down her plaid skirt over still shapely hips Mrs Forbes doesn't feel quite old enough for that yet anyway. Instead on these long afternoons she dreams, sometimes rehearsing a scene in which she receives news of her husband's unexpected death, sinking bonelessly into a handy chair, a handkerchief clutched in one hand the only sign of emotion. Having absorbed the shock but giving no hint of her true feelings (grief something that belonged behind closed doors) she sees herself as rising magnificently to the occasion, drawing on reserves of confidence and courage unsuspected by any of her friends . . . or indeed by her dead husband. Then, the funeral over (hers a lone figure following the coffin) she takes charge of her life, selling the house and moving into a flat, buying scarves and going to the theatre, life suddenly sunlit, roomy and accommodating.

Upstairs . . . and on the few occasions he wasn't round at his daughter-in-law's . . . Mr Forbes is finding release in scribbling notes on a saga of torture and rape in Renaissance Italy which he plans to work up on the internet for the benefit of another unseemly friend he has found for himself in Paterson, New Jersey.

People would have said this was a happy marriage, which it sort of was.

Mrs Forbes poured herself another sherry.

———

Having just completed a tour of the bank's east of England mortgages ripe for repossession Graham was driving through Peterborough when his phone rang.

'Hi, Toby. It's Gary. Where are you?'

'Peterborough.'

'Peterborough! Some people have all the luck. Having a good time?'

'No,' said Graham shortly.

'Why? It says here it has a Norman cathedral.'

Not being an imminent mortgage risk the cathedral had not figured in Graham's itinerary. 'How's the lady wife?'

'I can't hear,' said Graham. 'You're breaking up,' and he put the phone down.

Somewhere around Newark it rang again.

'Where are you?'

'About fifty miles north of where I was before and I'm not sure I like this.'

'Like what?'

'You calling me all the time.'

'All the time? Twice by my calculation. You should be flattered.'

'Why?' said Graham. 'I pay, remember.'

'That is crude. That is unworthy of you, Toby. A person has feelings.'

'Anyway,' said Graham, 'I can't today. I don't have any cash on me.'

'We could make it a freebie.'

Careful about money an offer like this would normally have appealed to Graham but even he could see that acceptance risked turning what was a transaction into a relationship.

'No. I've just found some in another pocket. Where shall I meet you?'

It was dark by the time Graham pulled alongside the waiting Gary in an empty car park, Kevin giving Toby a brief hug before walking him to the side door of a dark, oldish building where he punched in a code and let himself in.

'Where are you taking me?' said Graham as they walked down a bleak corridor lined with identical doors. It seemed to be some sort of hostel, the room

Gary let them into furnished with the bare essentials
. . . bed, washbasin, locker and with no evidence that
it was occupied even by Gary. It was suffocatingly hot.

'You've come down in the world,' said Graham.

'This?' said Kevin mildly as he took his trousers
off. 'No. It's the workplace.'

'And what were the other places? The luxury
apartment? The house in Roundhay?'

'They were the workplace too.'

'What do you do?' said Graham.

'I told you. I'm a panel beater.'

Putting his shoes neatly by the side of the bed
Graham noted the dust and fluff on the floor. 'Aren't
you going to lock the door?' said Graham.

'What for? There's nobody else here.'

Some clients might have been turned on by the
institutional nature of the surroundings but not
Graham.

'Where are we?' he said.

'I've told you. Work. Take your shirt off.'

Reflecting that he was the one who was supposed
to be calling the tune Graham nevertheless took it

off and his pants too. Unsurprisingly it was a less satisfactory session than they had had in the past, at one point even getting acrimonious when Graham drew the line, and quite early on in the proceedings Graham resolved that however keen Gary was this wasn't going to happen again.

Gary was leaning on his elbow while Graham lay on his back.

'What are you thinking about?' said Kevin.

Graham was actually thinking how much, other things being equal, he preferred his safe, cosy marital bed but he had the sense not to say so. He was also wondering how long it had to be before he could decently take his leave. Though before that there was the question of payment.

'How's married life?'

'Fine.'

'How's the bank?'

'The bank is fine.'

Kevin considered.

'Tell me. Does your mother know you're gay?'

'I'm married. That's all she knows.'

Graham reached for his shirt and started to put his clothes on though Kevin seemed in no hurry to do the same.

'They're always supposed to know, mothers.'

'You don't know mine.'

'True,' said Kevin, 'but what if she were to find out?'

'How would she do that? How much do I owe you? Same as last time?'

'How much do you love your mother?'

Graham stood, money in hand.

'What sort of a question is that? How much do you love your mother?'

'My mother knows.'

Graham had had enough of this.

'Same as before then?' and he put down some notes.

Kevin looked at them distastefully.

'Oh, I think we should say more than that. This is your mother, after all.'

'Oh no,' said Graham. 'Oh no,' and he picked up the money and put it back in his wallet.

'I'm not having truck with any of that. Any of that and I'll go straight to the police.'

'Very sensible,' said Kevin, hands clasped behind his head. 'And you wouldn't have far to go. I am the police. Now, take your clothes off and before we talk business perhaps we could reconsider the proposal I made you earlier.'

Graham had meant it when he had said he would go to the police and an hour later when he had made his escape he considered going straightaway. He then thought he should sleep on it and ideally talk it over with Betty. Sensible though this was it was obviously out of the question and in the event a week or two passed before, steeling himself for the inevitable embarrassment, he took steps to report the culprit.

The police station was unexpectedly civilised, tubs of geraniums on the doorstep with automatic doors sliding open on a bland reception area, a print by Van Gogh on one wall and one by Lowry on another, the ambience saying more about customer satisfaction than it did about law enforcement.

The desk sergeant, a kindly looking figure with white hair, was already dealing with a woman at the counter.

'I'm just seeing to this client but I shan't be a moment.' He indicated the reception area. 'Take a seat. There's coffee on the go though you've just missed the croissants.'

He turned back to the woman.

'Now what was he like?'

'Who?'

'The gentleman who assaulted you. Did you notice if he was black at all?'

The reassuring atmosphere notwithstanding Graham was still nervous and went in search of the loo.

This, too, turned out to be surprisingly upmarket with distant music that Betty though not Graham would have been able to identify as *The Lark Ascending*.

Then someone had been thoughtful enough to position a bowl of potpourri on the window sill, another touch which, had Graham not been preoccupied, would surely have got a tick.

As he came out the desk sergeant was just finishing with his customer while a woman PC waited to take charge.

'And shall I put you down for counselling?'

'What do you think?'

'It's good to talk,' said PC Valerie and took her off down the corridor.

'We can't always solve the crime,' said the sergeant, 'but at least we can make it easier to bear. Now, sir. Sorry to have kept you waiting. How can we help?'

Graham had decided to come straight to the point.

'The thing is,' and he leaned confidentially over the counter, 'it's a bit difficult. While I'm not exactly gay and am in fact happily married I've got myself into a bit of a fix and I'm being blackmailed.'

'Dear me,' said the desk sergeant. 'There's no need for that in this day and age. Blackmail! We aren't living in the 1950s. Well, you're in luck. I happen to know our community liaison officer is on the premises and you can have a little chat with him. I shan't keep you a moment.' And he went off down the corridor saying, 'Blackmail! Dear oh dear.'

Heartened by his sympathetic reception and relieved at the prospect of sharing his troubles Graham resumed his seat in the reception area where he idly leafed through some of the literature scattered about the low table. Turning a page of the local bulletin he came upon a photograph of a young policeman, looking shy but fetching in his uniform as he was being presented with an award for services to the community. It was Gary.

Not having kept abreast of liberation and its advancements Graham was slightly startled to find the award had been given to Gary (whose name appeared to be Kevin) for services to the community and in particular in his capacity as gay liaison officer. Having come out himself, 'as a policeman, an act of great personal courage', Kevin/Gary had been giving talks in schools, churches and to community groups, and was thought to be personally responsible for a significant fall in hate crime in the neighbourhood.

He was about to read on when somewhere down the corridor a door opened and Graham heard the sound of voices. Not daring to look back or to check who it was Graham ran down the steps, waiting an agonised second or two before the doors slid open and he could flee the premises.

It is a few days later and Betty is dawdling over her computer.

'Did you ever wonder', she said, 'whether Graham might be gay?'

Mr Forbes senior put on his glasses and considered.

'It had occurred to me,' he said, 'only then he married you so I assumed I must be mistaken.'

It was the afternoon and they were in bed.

'What about you?'

'It worried me', said Betty 'that he spent so much time on his fingernails, although men do moisturise nowadays, don't they?'

'They do,' agreed Mr Forbes (who didn't). 'He was always fastidious even as a boy and he had an umbrella at a very early age. Still, I wouldn't worry about it. He likes you, that's the main thing.'

'Yes,' said Betty, 'but he is gay. I've known for a while.' (She'd followed up some of the websites he'd been visiting.) 'I was just bothered that you didn't.'

'Is it a problem?' said his father.

'Not as such,' said Betty. 'And he does very well.'

'Which just leaves Muriel,' said Mr Forbes. 'There'd be a problem there.'

'Has she made any progress on the computer?'

'What do you think?' said Mr Forbes.

Betty frowned, her fingers scampering over the keys.

'What's the matter?'

Betty shook her head as she brought Graham's personal account up on the screen. 'I can't work it out. He's been making some very odd payments.'

Though Graham and (as he was still bound to call him) Gary now met regularly Graham never mentioned his visit to the police station or that he knew of Kevin's respected position in the community . . . a role which even Graham could see rendered him as vulnerable to blackmail as his victim. How, though, could he turn the tables? Short of coming out and telling Betty and his mother for the moment there was nothing to be done.

A casualty of the heightened commerciality of the relationship between the two men was any pleasure Graham might have been expected to glean from their connection. He did what he was told glumly and with no joy, never able to forget that he was being physically humiliated and was paying for the privilege besides with, most injured, his pride.

His marked lack of enthusiasm, while entirely understandable, still managed to irk his tormentor who felt that some minimal rapture was owing. But it was not forthcoming and Graham was not a good enough actor to simulate it.

'The spoilsport,' thought Kevin. Still, and he trousered another grand, there were compensations.

In time, though, boredom took its toll even on Kevin and more and more when they met money changed hands but nothing else.

The hangover from these unwilling trysts affected Betty, too. The exuberance that had made Graham such an enlivening partner was now virtually extinguished. He came to bed and went to sleep, but often now she would wake in the night and find him awake too.

At first Betty thought this was what was to be expected, the shine going off the marriage as it was supposed to do. But there were other more disturbing developments. Undressing, Graham had always put his clothes neatly on or over the back of the chair, his shoes, socks inside, tucked cosily under the bed. This new Graham now left his shirt on the floor and his shoes all over the place so that Betty wondered at first if he was having a breakdown before deciding he wasn't imaginative enough for that.

Something was wrong, though, and his fingernails were a disgrace.

Chaste as their life together had become, it was not wanting in affection. Indeed since Graham's trouble he had become a far kinder and more considerate and appealing person than he had ever been before. He came to his wife for comfort and reassurance though over what he was never specific. 'Life' was the nearest he got to it.

'Is it work?' Betty asked.

'Not really.'

'You're not ill?'

He shook his head mutely.

'You're so good to me,' he would mumble before drifting off to troubled sleep. Tonight, though, he lay awake and talked about their future, saying he didn't want to spend the rest of his life in a bank and had she ever thought of Australia.

Betty had never thought of Australia, being quite happy with Alwoodley. So she was about to 'talk it through' as he put it when Graham leaped out of bed and peered through the curtains.

'What is it?'

'Nothing,' said Graham. 'I thought there was a car outside.'

At first,' said Betty, 'I thought he was just stealing from the bank, only why I couldn't think as there's always plenty of money in his account.'

They were in bed again, the laptop eponymously open on her lap, Mr Forbes reading.

She didn't say this to Mr Forbes but what shocked Betty wasn't the peculation itself; it was that the amounts involved, while not trivial, were relatively small. Acquisitive though Graham was and bold though he thought himself he had always been modest in his aspirations and limited in his ambitions, how limited he himself had never appreciated. He had never realised, for instance, that what he took to be Betty's fortune was actually only the accumulated interest from her real fortune which lay elsewhere. In the light of this the amounts that Graham was embezzling from the bank were negligible, but they would need to be repaid and repaid quickly before an audit showed them up.

Actually she was doing Graham an injustice. He was modest in his assumptions, it's true, but so, too, was Kevin and it was his demands that dictated the withdrawals, each as limited in his expectations as the other.

'So where is the money going?' said Mr Forbes.

'Give me five minutes,' said Betty.

Simpler, of course, would have been to ask the man

himself, 'Are you being blackmailed?' but several considerations made this course of action unfeasible. For
a start it blew Betty's cover as the simple but adoring
wife, knowing nothing of money or accounts or the
world in general. Bad enough that she would have to
reveal that she had been poring over his bank state-
ments and in the process had sufficient know-how
to spot payments that were dubious or inexplicable;
but more generally undesirable in Betty's view would
be the transformation of their relationship that must
come about were Graham to realise she knew that he
was gay (if even occasionally). Lacking in intellec-
tual stimulation though it was, their set-up seemed
to Betty pretty well satisfactory. The adjustments
consequent on either of them coming clean were too
radical (and too tedious) even to contemplate . . . his
bluster, her forbearance, no: cards on tables was not
a solution. 'I've found him,' said Betty . . .

Graham's mother was just thinking of having an early sherry when the doorbell went. It was a policeman.

'Good afternoon, Mrs Forbes. I am the Crime

Prevention Officer. There has been a spate of burg-
laries in the neighbourhood and we're conducting a
survey of home security.'

He showed her an identity card.

'May I come in?'

'Of course.'

But then he didn't, just waiting on the doorstep.

'No offence, Mrs Forbes, but you have already
made two mistakes. One, you opened the door
straightaway without putting it on the chain before
ascertaining who the caller might be. Two, you didn't
even look at my identification. Check it out.'

He showed it to her again and she looked more
carefully. It was a card for a swimming club, the
policeman . . . if he was a policeman . . . half-naked
in swimming trunks.

'It's a lovely photo,' said Mrs Forbes, 'but it's not
the legal one.'

'Quite so,' said the Crime Prevention Officer. 'You
sometimes have to commit crimes in order to prevent
them. This is the one you should have been shown,'
and he handed her another card with a (clothed this

time) photograph and which attested to his status as
Crime Prevention Officer.

'Now, Mrs Forbes, having established my cre-
dentials, may I come in?'

'Certainly,' said Mrs Forbes. 'I was just going to
have some tea.'

'He could have been anybody,' said Mr Forbes later.

'Yes. He told me that, only I know a policeman
when I see one. And if you're so concerned for my
well-being you should try being at home more often.
How long does it take to put up a shelf?'

'The shelves are finished, I'm doing the draught
excluders now.'

'What did he look like?' said Graham.

'Very handsome,' said his mother. 'He showed
me a picture of him in swimming trunks.'

'The policeman? What on earth for?'

'To test me. Then he showed me the proper one with
his clothes on. He's the Crime Prevention Officer.'

'So you keep saying. What did you tell him?'

'I didn't have to tell him anything. He knew it all. It's on the internet, apparently.'

'The internet?'

'The computer. One of those things.'

'What you don't realise', said Graham, 'is that now I'm higher up in the bank we're all much more vulnerable. Bankers' families get kidnapped on a regular basis as a way of getting into the safe.'

'Not in Alwoodley, surely. I said to him, I don't like the police knowing all our details and he said it was just to be on the safe side. Though he had one or two things wrong. He thought your name was Toby. I said, "Toby?" I said you'd once had a dog called Toby when you were little, do you remember? that smelly little article that we had to get rid of . . . that was the only Toby I knew. We laughed.'

'Nice woman your mother,' said Kevin. 'Adores you.'

'Yes,' said Graham. 'That's the only reason I'm here.'

It was another bleak car park.

'Shame you got married, though. She wasn't expecting that.'

'Leave her alone.'

'I beg your pardon.'

'What's my mother got to do with you? I'm paying, aren't I? Leave her alone.'

'I have to do my duty. The premises are inadequately protected. They don't even have an alarm bell.'

So in due course Mrs Forbes senior's policeman made what he called 'a follow-up visit', bringing the homeowner the latest literature on laser technology in the service of crime prevention. She had poured him a sherry and they were in the lounge discussing where, should she invest in some sensors, they could best be positioned. His standing on a chair to point out the preferred locations gave Mrs Forbes a chance to admire the same well-muscled back that her son had had occasion to stroke the fateful night before his wedding. Now, though, it was filling out a crisp white uniform shirt, set off by epaulettes, a pager thrust into the back pocket.

'And all this advice is free?' said Mrs Forbes.

'Absolutely, because from the police point of view, it pays for itself. The more secure the premises the fewer the break-ins.

'Mrs Forbes,' said the policeman.

'Please,' said Mrs Forbes, 'call me Muriel . . .' And she put her hand on his knee.

When an hour or so later Mr Forbes let himself in it was to find the householder and the Crime Prevention Officer both on the sofa where she was showing him the photograph albums with pictures of Graham as a boy.

'That's Toby,' she said pointing to a scruffy Scotty cradled in the boy's arms. 'Dreadful dog. Always rolling in things.'

'Does he know Graham?' said Mr Forbes after the policeman had gone.

'Know him?' said Mrs Forbes. 'Why should he? He's a policeman.'

Having had a good look round a different car park, this one multi-storey, Kevin kept it under surveillance for at least an hour before suddenly slipping into the passenger seat beside Betty. 'How can I help you?'

'I'm Graham's wife.'

'Is that why you're crying? Though I have to say I don't know any Grahams. Do you mean Toby?'

'Possibly.' Betty blew her nose.

'If his name is Graham why does he call himself Toby?'

'How much do you want?' said Betty. 'I mean, to call it a day?'

Ten minutes later their talk satisfactorily concluded Kevin got out of the car.

On the other side of the car park Mr Forbes took another photograph and switched off his recording machine.

'Nice doing business with you,' said Kevin. Which is not what he said when a copy of the CD came through the letter box next morning.

'We do lead an exciting life,' said Mr Forbes as they drove home. 'It never used to be like this.' So now the phone calls abruptly and inexplicably ceased and with no word from his sometime tormentor Graham's marital vigour reasserted itself and, his fingernails once more immaculate, life returned to its old ways. It puzzled Graham that there was no comeback at the bank and when he eventually came to look into it he could find no trace in the accounts that anything had ever been wrong. When something bothered him at work he would normally talk it over with Betty, which in this case he couldn't do so for a while he remained uneasy, eventually deciding that Kevin being a policeman this had led him . . . or the force possibly . . . to make the necessary reimbursement just for safety's sake.

Mrs Forbes, the unwitting beneficiary of the thwarted blackmail, remains unwitting, ignorant both of the peculations of her son and the ingenuity of her daughter-in-law who, along with her husband, were concerned only to safeguard her innocence.

Such concern might be thought of as wholly admirable except that self-servingness comes into it, too, and a distaste for disturbance and the attach-

71

ment of all these parties to a landscape that is familiar and which the convulsive revelation of her son's sexuality would certainly reshape.

There was, too . . . and this may be harder to understand . . . there was affection. Monstrous as she was, a tyrant and a snob, Graham's mother was an ogre of such long-standing that her feelings (though they could often only be guessed at) nevertheless merited respect. Not yet an ancient monument she was a survival and on that score alone her outlook and her armour-plated ignorance merited preservation.

None of this would have found much sympathy with the lady in question, the object of these elaborate precautions almost certainly viewing such consideration as neither necessary nor appropriate. Graham's mother did not need shielding from the knowledge that her beloved son was homosexual: she had known it all along. It was an opinion she had never bothered to share with her husband but before Betty had come into their lives she had always thought Graham 'not the marrying sort' and it was one of her (unspoken) grievances against Betty that the marriage had made it necessary for her to revise that opinion.

So when Kevin, in a last shot of his bolt (and more out of pique than self-interest), came round one afternoon and spilled the (long-postponed) beans Mrs Forbes was relieved rather than surprised: it was a return to the natural order of things. She had been right all along. True she put on a good amateur performance of what she imagined a devastated mother's reaction might be, staring hard and grim-jawed out of the window as she contemplated the wreck of all her hopes, a performance so convincing it impelled Kevin to lay a consoling hand on her shoulder.

This was a mistake.

She poured them both a sherry. Looking at this delightful young man she could hardly blame her son who had, after all, impeccable taste. Marriage to someone as unprepossessing as Betty had been a lapse, which, thankfully, had only been temporary, the implication being that what a man needed in a woman (and which Mrs Forbes saw herself as providing) was perfection: given anything less a chap such as Graham was not to be blamed if he washed his hands of the whole gender and shopped elsewhere.

'Can you blame him?' she said to the captive Kevin. 'It takes a woman to understand.'

Carried to its logical conclusion, of course, this free-market theory of sexual preference is hardly tenable as it would see the ranks of deviance swollen by droves of disappointed normality. Not that Mrs Forbes cares about that, her thoughts for the moment busy with a more immediate breach of suburban rectitude.

In conclusion, how much better . . . how much *healthier* . . . had all these persons, these family members, been more candid with one another right from the start.

As it is there's every chance Betty will grow bored with Graham, with divorce the obvious solution. Except that they now have twins, whom they both adore, and besides divorce might mean that some awkward truths would have to be told and neither of them wants that.

That Mr Forbes still from time to time sleeps with his daughter-in-law and leads a vigorous fantasy life on the internet besides would shame both his wife and his son did it ever come to light; but why should it, the only clue to their clandestine relationship Betty's disproportionate grief on Mr Forbes's death from a heart attack a few years later? The death of her husband while at last giving Mrs Forbes occasion to play for real her often-rehearsed scene of sudden bereavement also draws Graham and his mother closer together, much as they had been before his marriage. Then, having had one sherry too many and thinking the better to bond with her boy and to show him she's still in the game, Mrs Forbes comes clean on her escapade with Kevin. It had been more short-lived than she let on, their brief relationship curtailed when, a few months later, Kevin perished in a high-speed motorway car chase, a death that might seem to have more to do with narrative tidiness than any driving without due care and attention. Far from drawing him closer to his mother the revelation of this liaison, however perfunctory, shocks and embarrasses Graham, who feels that his mother might have had the consideration to keep this distasteful news to herself. It also abuts far too closely on his own sexual preferences, still, he fondly imagines, a secret known only to himself.

Graham goes home and tells Betty about Mrs Forbes and her fling with Kevin, 'this gay policeman' as Graham describes him. Betty, who, unsurprisingly, is unsurprised, promises never to tell a soul, the souls she particularly must not tell the twins. She also mustn't tell them what Graham still hasn't told her, namely that their father is not as other men are and likely to go on being so. Though if he'd told her that in the first place he would never have married her and there would be no story.

But the most secret secret of all which Betty alone knows is that the father of the twins is probably their grandfather.

So the secrets abound, with Betty more richly endowed with them as she is with everything else. Still, for all that everybody, while not happy, is not unhappy about it. And so they go on.